Let It Grow

A Play by

Chad Henderson

Let It Grow

A Play by

Chad Henderson

The Play Right Series

LET IT GROW
Copyright © 2024 by Chad Henderson

All rights reserved. Printed in the United States of America. No parts of this publication may be reproduced in any manner without written permission except in the case of brief quotations embodied in critical analyses and reviews.

For stock or amateur performance rights, contact the playwright through his website at chadhendersondirects.com.

Library of Congress Number: 2024943842

ISBN: 978-1-942081-41-8

A publication of The Jasper Project an imprint of Muddy Ford Press Chapin, SC

All printed and online media related to subsequent performances and development of this play, in perpetuity, must state the following: *Let It Grow* by Chad Henderson was developed via The Jasper Project's Play Right Series in the summer of 2024 in Columbia, SC, USA.

The Play Right Series

JasperProject.org

The Play Right Series

The purpose of the Jasper Project's Play Right Series is to:

Empower and enlighten audiences by allowing them insider views of the processes of creating theatre art;

Increase opportunities for theatre artists to create and participate in new art without the necessity of being attached to an existing theatre organization; and to

Provide more affordable and experimental theatre arts experiences for new and emerging theatre artists and their audiences; thereby expanding cultural literacy and theatre arts appreciation in the South Carolina Midlands.

FOREWORD

Judging this book by its cover, you would assume it contains a play about love, loss and plants set on a familiar public television gardening show. Fair enough. But now ask yourself some questions:

- How do you mend a broken heart?
- Where is the line between your private self and your public self, and who gets to draw it?
- Are our attempts to make the world more comfortable making it less so?
- Is Nickelback all that bad?
- Where, on a scale of Mimosa Pudica to Common Stinkhorn, would you rate your emotional availability?
- Does Dolly Parton sleep on her back?

If you have answers to those, good on you. You're obviously an introspective person. If you don't, welcome to the right place: Chad Henderson's marvelous *Let It Grow*. As do many good plays, Chad's lulls us into a sense of security simply by showing us a good time, but then, before our astonished eyes, blossoms to unveil the many layers on which it's been operating the entire time.

Who could know our favorite gardening show is actually a microcosm of the larger world beset by conflicts and imperatives—moral, financial, romantic and political? *Let It Grow* is just what its reader needs to do: allow it the time and sunlight it needs to foliate, and then behold it in full-flower. Do that and you'll find yourself agreeing with local theatrical luminary Darion McCloud, who calls *Let It Grow* "a surprising bit of tender," and adds, "Bravo!"

Chad's name is likely familiar to you. He was for six years the producing Artistic Director at Trustus Theatre, in which capacity he carved out a place for himself as one of the Midlands' foremost artistic movers and shakers. He has also taken theatrical projects to theaters in Charleston, Spartanburg, and Key West. In 2017, his short film *Overture* won the

Audience Award in Jasper's Second Act Film Festival. At present, he is the Marketing Director for the South Carolina Philharmonic. If you already know all that, good on you. You're obviously a fascinating person.

And if you're a Jasper Project regular, you're perhaps already aware that *Let It Grow* is the fourth play developed, presented and published by its Play Right Series. The first was Randall David Cook's *Sharks and Other Lovers* (2017), which went on to full production at Greenville's Center Stage. Next came Colby Quick's *Moon Swallower* (2022), which has been produced at USC Aiken and, rumor has it, has another production in the works, as does our third play, Lonetta Thompson's *Therapy* (2023).

The Series was created to connect theater creators with consumers, to support the state's playwrights, whose successes are a constant source of our delight, and to reward the advocacy and investment of our Actor Sponsors and Community Producers who each year make the whole thing possible. If you are or have been one of them, good on us. We're so grateful for you.

– Jon Tuttle
   September, 2024

PREFACE

"If I could, I'd relive those days
I know the one thing that would never change"

– ~~William Shakespeare~~, Chad Kroeger, Nickelback, from "Photograph"

This play is ultimately a story about the power of grace. There are a lot of definitions for that word provided by the kind AI entities at Merriam-Webster dot com. I looked it up just now, and when I cite "grace" I'm referring specifically to: "the disposition to or an act or instance of kindness, courtesy, or clemency" and/or "a temporary exemption."

I also looked up "preface" to see how the robots would direct me, and they reported back with: "the introductory remarks of a speaker or author." Well, that's no help when trying to come up with something poignant to offer you as you set sail into these pages.

I will be honest with you, dear reader, and let you know that I have not mastered the act of grace. I certainly have not mastered the act of writing a preface, as you are literally experiencing right now.

I wrote this play in the company of my plants and cats. I generally wrote it when my wife was working, because...I mean...why would I sit around writing a play when I could be hanging out with her? For real.

Finally, please note that I had to also look up the lyrics to a Nickelback song, because I thought it'd be a funny introduction to this preface (once you read the play, you'll get it). I was a ska kid. I'm learned in the ways of a much more disparaged and humiliating style of music.

Anyway, here's the play...

– Chad Henderson
  September, 2024

Let It Grow was developed in conjunction with The Jasper Project's Play Right Series during the summer, 2024, and received a public staged reading at Harbison Theatre on September 14, 2024. Series judges were Libby Campbell-Turner, Kari Lebby and Dewey Scott-Wiley.

Actor Sponsors—a designation for those whose level of support was particularly significant—were Linda Khoury and William Schmidt. Community Producers were Cindi Boiter, Hunter Boyle, Robin Gottlieb, Billy Guess, Bob Jolley, Ed Madden, Bert Easter, Melanie McGehee, Adam McGehee, Jack McKenzie, and Wade Sellers.

Let It Grow was directed by Marybeth Gorman Craig. The cast was as follows:

Mary Lily	Libby Campbell-Turner
Jeb	David Britt
Charlotte	Kayla Machado
Christoph	G. Scott Wild

The "Let it Grow" theme was arranged by Andy Bell.

SETTING

The Present. The "Let It Grow" television studio, a program on South Carolina public television. In the studio is a garden coach desk, many plants, monitors, cozy decor and Mary Lily's office. All scenes that don't take place in the studio could be played downstage of the garden coach desk. Or whatever you conjure with a production team.

CHARACTERS

MARY	60s, "Let It Grow" creator and host
JEB	50s or 40s, longtime garden coach
CHARLOTTE	30s, co-producer and garden coach
CHRISTOPH	60s, celebrated author and new garden coach

SCENE I

A public television studio for the popular gardening show "Let It Grow," hosted by Mary Lily. The theme song plays, and it sounds a lot like a popular song from a cartoon about a snow queen. Mary and her longtime garden coach, Jeb Alethea, seem to be having an uncomfortable conversation as they get into place for the segment they're about to film. As the studio lights come up, they seem to be caught off-guard, but quickly transition into "show mode."

MARY

    Welcome back to "Let it Grow." We have such a treat for you this week, but in the matter of full disclosure: I have to admit that I am standing on a box. *(Mary steps down.)* This is the real Mary Lily right here. *(Jeb nervously laughs. Mary steps back up on her box.)* But Jeb brought such wonderful plants from his nursery, they're so vigorous and fun, that I wanted to stand up a little bit so we can enjoy them more. And Jeb, it is Native Plant Week here on the show, and I know you love to walk the woodlands along the Reedy River and find inspiration there and always have—but I wanted to talk about your new success with sustainable fertilization at your nursery.

JEB

    My new specialty, yes ma'am.

MARY

    Now I can tell by these beauties in front of us, that you can share a lot with us.

JEB

    Well, I do want to start out by saying that fertilizers and manure are only one small part of the plant wellness puzzle. But it can have a lot of benefits, especially when you're doing it in an ecological and sustainable way. That's why we want to talk about a common household resource that can add to the botanical beauty of the native plants in your garden.

MARY

Well, let's dive on into this scat-versation then and get into these plants, Jeb. Mercy, let's start with this large one over here. It's absolutely alluring.

JEB

It sure is. Well, this is Titi *(pronounces it 'teety'),* and Titi grows in the swamps.

MARY

Well, we traditionally pronounce it tie-tie don't we, and Cyrilla is the genus.

JEB

Yes, Titi is Cyrilla racemiflora. Sorry, I must have some nerves. Now, I've known Teety for a long time, and never seen a pretty one growing in a swamp. However, grown in the nursery setting, you can get quite an attractive shape.

MARY

The Titi can....

JEB

It can get a more graceful arching habit of growth if you let it. And it can be used as a great foundation plant.

MARY

I just love the Titi in my garden. I find that the blooms are so beautiful and welcome scandalous visitations from pollinators.

JEB

Yes mam, a Teety has been known to get a pollinator active.

MARY

(To camera) Tie-Tie. And to attract those pollinators you have to get it to grow beautifully, as you have done here.

JEB

Well the little magic trick we've got under our sleeves at Alethea Nursery is using Humanure—which is a sustainable resource.

MARY

Now, we all want to know a little more about that.

JEB

Of course. As you know, every time we flush waste down the toilet we are creating a toxic problem.

MARY

I'll be....

JEB

So with a compost toilet system you're able to capture that amazing resource and take care of it, and treat it in a way that removes any pathogens or problematic elements.

MARY

There are a lot of naturalists that believe this a basic fundamental thing we should all be doing.

JEB

I couldn't agree more. Why would you buy manure when you've got this resource right here? All we're essentially doing is doing our business in buckets, for lack of a better word, and covering it with a nice cover material—most usually old sawdust from the mill over to our nursery, it's already got a lot of good bacteria and fungus in it—

MARY

I'll bet!

JEB

—and then we hot compost it in a palate framed compost.

MARY

Now, we know that human scat can have pathogens like roundworm eggs and other kinds of worm eggs that can cause some serious problems for our plant friends....

JEB

Yes, and if you do a hot compost that's the safest way because you can nuke all of those things within hours.

MARY

Voila! And your entire staff is involved in this ecological compost initiative?

JEB

Yes mam, they are. And while we still have traditional toilets at the nursery for visitors and shoppers, we have found that many are willing to join us in creating sustainable nourishment for our plant friends—and the kids seem to think it's a real treat as well.

MARY

Well, that's just wonderful. And obviously your plants appreciate this effort because they seem to be singing "thank you, thank you," if you ask me.

JEB

Humanure will get them singing, yes ma'am. And we've also seen great results with these blueberries.

MARY

Zenobia. Zenobia pulverulenta. I do love these resilient shrubs. And blueberries are, of course, the go-to backyard fruit for so many.

JEB

It's great to use as a foundation—and its evergreen.

MARY

These berries seem to be singing as well, just loving the care they're receiving at your nursery.

JEB

I'll let them sing for themselves.

(Jeb plucks a few berries and hands them to Mary. They eat them.)

MARY

It's as if Beethoven himself is sitting at a little piano in my mouth, and he's composing "Ode to Joy." So flavorful.

JEB

We'll give that a "Bravo" then.

MARY

We always appreciate you sharing all that you know with us, Jeb. And what fun that you could step away from the panel to teach us so much today. Thank you.

JEB

Thank you, always a pleasure.

MARY

And we'll see you all next week, and until then—have fun letting it grow!

CHARLOTTE

(From offstage:) And we're out!

(Lights shift as the show is over. We hear the closing credits music from the control room. Jeb immediately changes his posture and demeanor, leaning over the table. Mary seems to deflate as well. This has not been a fun shoot. Charlotte enters. She is the newly appointed assistant producer, and is also a regular garden coach on the show.)

CHARLOTTE

Alright good. Nice job, Jeb. And Mary, love, good show as always.

MARY

Thank you, dear. Well done.

CHARLOTTE

Here, let me get a post-show picture real quick for the socials.

MARY

Oh, do you have to be so close up, Charlotte?

CHARLOTTE

We gotta do this stuff so we can tag the sponsors.

MARY

I guess they're running the show now. Brave new world. Well, just back off a teensie bit for me. Come here Jeb.

(Mary wraps her arms around Jeb and smiles as Charlotte takes picture. Jeb suddenly burps because he almost gags.)

CHARLOTTE

OK. You take care of whatever that is Jeb. Gotta get your mics.

(Charlotte helps Mary and Jeb remove mics throughout the following. Jeb rights himself, then looks to Mary.)

JEB

If you don't replace Dale soon, I'm gonna quit.

MARY

Please don't make this any harder than it already is.

JEB

Hell, why ain't Dale here anyway?

MARY

I can't do anything about the fact that he crashed into Studio B right before we needed to start taping this season.

JEB

Well, people tuned in for him. And I didn't sign up to do these damn Act III presentations. I'm the manure slash fertilization guru, and I talk about gettin' the right shit in your garden. I do it at the table where we all talk at the top of the show. I ain't supposed to sit here and flap my damn gums with you in a feature segment. It gets me sick. I got the bubble-gut so bad, I think if I leaned over I could paint the side of a barn.

MARY

Well, I didn't know it would make ya that nervous.

CHARLOTTE

You've been a garden coach for so long.

JEB

Maybe I better go shit in the creek out there so we don't catch the woods on fire.

MARY

Jeb, I'm sorry 'bout it all, but you did great, okay?

JEB

Guess I just don't like coming in here and being told by Charlotte that I'm in a segment I didn't expect. It makes me madder than a one-legged diabetic at a cake walk.

CHARLOTTE

You know, if you showed up more than two minutes before taping, maybe you'd get the information in time to process instead of getting all flustered.

JEB

I didn't mean to make a scene....

CHARLOTTE

Well, you did fine. You won't have to do it ever again. My God....

MARY

We're going to have someone new in here as soon as possible, Jeb.

CHARLOTTE

Yes, I'm working on it. Everyone should know I'm working on it. I don't see why everyone can't just let me do what I'm hired to do.

MARY

You okay, dear?

CHARLOTTE

Yes. Sorry. Just a little overwhelmed with all of it. And he's not helping.

MARY

Well, let's just all try to count to ten then. I know you can handle this.

JEB

And I'll be quiet.

CHARLOTTE

That'll be the day.

(Charlotte, done with getting the mics, exits.)

JEB

Tell me straight, what happened to Dale?

MARY

He...well, I guess he messed up too much.

JEB

The crash?

MARY

Well, the crash. Maybe the thing at the bar the week before that?

JEB

He got into a little bar brawl, that's all.

MARY

I'm not disagreeing....

JEB

Aw hell, I can't tell you how many times somebody's opened up a smart mouth. I've told some fellers in the past year that they better shit in their momma's best frying pan than to mess with me, cause I'd fold 'em up like a fourth grade love letter. Legal ain't letting *me* go over it.

MARY

This bar fight was at the station's fundraising gala, and it was with a sponsor from that kids' show, and your quibbles weren't front page news like that wreck, either.

JEB

And they just let him go....

MARY

I know. Dale's just going through so much. I hate it for him.

JEB

It wasn't three good enough strikes if you ask me. The damn Legal.

MARY

Yeah, they get a lot of say now, whether we like it or not. I'm going to miss watching you two cut up.

JEB

Yeah, me too. Just sounds like he needed a talking to rather than losing his livelihood. He was going through the shit. And we've all got to go through the shit from time to time.

MARY

They let him go at the University too.

JEB

So...absolutely nobody gave the man a chance? Is that what you're saying?

MARY

Legal said we had to let him go after the crash. Liability and all that. It's not the way I used to run things, but I guess that's how they're being run.

(Charlotte enters.)

CHARLOTTE

We ready to get out? Let's get a drink. Floor staff is going to be ready to shut down soon.

JEB

Well, color me flabbergasted. Charlotte wants to go find a happy hour.

CHARLOTTE

It's been a helluva two weeks.

JEB

I couldn't agree more. I'm in. *(To Mary:)* How about you?

MARY

I'm going to record the radio spots for tomorrow. But ya'll go on and have a lovely time.

JEB

Don't sit around here too late. I know how you are when you get behind that mic. *(Pause.)* Hey, you okay?

MARY

Just going to record my spots.

JEB

Okay. I just know what today is. And I know there's a lot going on with the show, but I just gotta check in on my Ms. Mary, you know.

MARY

I miss him today and every day, Jeb, and that isn't going to change. But I'm all right. Charlotte's taken so much off my plate. She's producing now, and doing a good job, huh?

JEB

Yeah, I think so.

MARY

(To Charlotte) I mean it…you can believe me, dear.

(Charlotte hugs Mary.)

CHARLOTTE

Thanks, love. Dixon's?

JEB

Dixon's it is.

CHARLOTTE

Bye Mary. Oh, and if you get a chance, shoot yourself when you record the radio spots. You can put them on our stories.

MARY

Shoot myself?

CHARLOTTE

With your phone. I made you an admin on everything.

MARY

My mother had some sort of saying about being in films that would be seen by strangers, but I can't recall it at present.

CHARLOTTE

I can help you with it later if you want.

MARY

Oh, yes, 'get the money first' was the advice. That was it. Well, ya'll be good.

JEB

Bye Mary. *(Back to Charlotte: as they exit:)* I hope Billy is bartending. That boy ain't got walkin' around sense. I asked him for a Icehouse five times, and he still came back every time cause he couldn't remember. It's like the wheel's spinning but the hamster's dead. Makes me laugh. I'm riding with you. *(He turns and screams out to house:)* Hey! You interns get them plants out to my truck. Welcome to "Let It Grow"!

(Jeb and Charlotte laugh and exit while the lights shut down for the night. Mary pulls out her phone and looks at it, shakes her head, then heads to her office.)

SCENE II

Another show day. Mary and Charlotte are talking.

CHARLOTTE

One of our new sponsors is here today. Mr. Goldstein. He owns the Gardener's Warehouse. He's just gonna trail around with me so you don't have to bother with him.

MARY

Now, you should introduce me when he gets here, so I can let him know we do so appreciate his support.

CHARLOTTE

I will when we get a chance. Now remember, we'll roll that segment you did over at the Japanese Gardens in Newberry for Act III.

MARY

We got the year on it?

CHARLOTTE

We've got the year on it, don't worry, love. I'm looking after things. You should go get your outfit on.

MARY

You don't want me in sweats?

CHARLOTTE

You wear whatever you want. It's your show.

MARY

I'm just kidding, dear. Better go put my duds on.

(Mary heads to her office. Jeb enters the studio.)

JEB

    Hell, goddamighty it's hot out there. I saw a damn bear picking up a fish with oven mitts.

CHARLOTTE

    Morning Jeb. Hope you ate, the catering is late.

JEB

    I already supped, thank you. Had to eat 'cause I was working on that truck. I flipped the engine this morning, and it was knocking like a Jehovah's witness. I laid under that truck all morning trying to get it fixed.

CHARLOTTE

    Did you get it fixed?

JEB

    Do you see me showing up well before filming?

CHARLOTTE

    You took an Uber didn't you?

JEB

    I did.

CHARLOTTE

    You settle in while I go check in on the booth, and I'll come back and walk you through today's script....

JEB

Yes mam. Gonna rest my damn feet. I feel like a shit sandwich without the bread.

CHARLOTTE

Okay.

(Charlotte exits. Jeb sits in his usual chair at the panel. Christoph enters though the stage door, wanders closer to Jeb.)

JEB

Damn. Laying under that truck got my ass and feet howlin'. Betsy's going to say it's a circulation issue, but she's always got ailments for me, and nary a certificate of medical accomplishment to speak of....

(Jeb takes his shoe off to investigate. Christoph approaches Jeb.)

CHRISTOPH

Hey there, Mr. James Alethea? I love watching you on the show.

JEB

Yessir, and I thank you. But listen, the catering usually comes in that front door. The door you entered through so casually says "Stage Door"— so I'm supposin' maybe you think you own the place? Well, no bother —the red light wasn't on, so I guess it mighaswellabeen green.

CHRISTOPH

Oh, I'm sorry? I'm not a caterer. I don't even know how to cook, really.

JEB

    Sir, even though I don't know who you are, it's a strange world when a civilian enters through a door clearly marked "Stage Door." On a brief inventory, this action would indicate an unfortunate diagnosis of a devil-may-care way-of-livin'. Did you arrive on a motorcycle with your taste for personal freedom?

(Mary enters from office with new shirt. Sees Christoph, obviously the new sponsor?)

CHRISTOPH

    I drove a Subaru.

JEB

    So you just like poppin' up into television studios?

MARY

    (Taking over:) Well hello there. I'm Mary Lily, the show's host.

CHRISTOPH

    Yes, Ms. Lily. It is an honor to meet you.

MARY

    No, the pleasure is all ours. We're always so glad to have our treasured supporters join us for a taping. You've met Mr. Alethea I see.

JEB

    /Supporter...oh....

CHRISTOPH

    I did. Very good to meet you officially. Been a fan for sometime.

JEB

(Suddenly in show mode:) And it is a pleasure to meet you Mr...?

CHRISTOPH

Marion. I'm Christoph Marion.

(They all shake hands.)

MARY

Christoph Marion?

JEB

Christoph? What happened to the rest of the name?

CHRISTOPH

I'm sorry...?

MARY

You're Christoph Marion?

JEB

Well, it's like Christopher without the ending, or like music and acting legend Kris Kristofferson, without the ever-pleasant "-offerson" as a finale to the name, which really draws the name together, if you ask me....

MARY

I didn't realize you'd be joining us today, Mr. Marion. Jeb gets nervous when he meets new folks.

JEB

I guess I do get nerves. Like a blind man in a fish market.

CHRISTOPH

I don't follow...?

JEB

Well, if you're like blind, you know, and you walk into a fish market. It could be like "Mmkay, we got fish here." Or you could be like "maybe I walked in here and it's a brothel with no hygiene policies" or something like that. Either way, better have a bit of folding money, am I right? I don't think before I speak.

(Charlotte enters to greet Christoph.)

CHARLOTTE

Mr. Marion, we're so glad you're finally on set!

CHRISTOPH

Good to be here.

CHARLOTTE

Christoph is our new garden coach and he'll do some segments too.

MARY

Welcome, welcome, welcome! My goodness, I would have liked to have known you were joining us. But it seems Charlotte decided to keep the host in the dark.

CHARLOTTE

There were just a lot of spinning plates....

MARY

The feeling of foolishness will pass, but at first, I thought you were our new sponsor!

CHARLOTTE

No, that's Mr. Goldstein from the Gardener's Warehouse. I told you. He's in the booth right now. You can wave.

(They all look to the booth and wave slowly.)

MARY

I thought you were going to introduce us.

CHARLOTTE

He just got here.

JEB

(Through his smile:) Have they been able to hear us the whole time?

CHARLOTTE

No...your mics are off.

JEB

Well, shit fire and save matches.

CHARLOTTE

Christoph, we gotta get you mic'd up because we're about to get started. Here we go. *(Charlotte mics Christoph up very quickly as they all get into their places for filming.)* Now you remember what we talked about?

CHRISTOPH

I do...yes. Still nervous.

CHARLOTTE

Don't worry, Mary runs the whole thing. She's been doing this for thirty years. And it's the second day of filming so you'll just slide right into it.

MARY

Mr. Marion, I am so glad you're our new garden coach.

CHRISTOPH

Please call me Christoph.

MARY

I must've read *Fifty Shades of Stamens* three times in one sitting.

CHARLOTTE

It was certainly attention-grabbing....

(Charlotte is done with mic and sits at the panel with her computer.)

CHRISTOPH

Well, I really do / thank you for that...

JEB

Fifty Shades of Stamens? That was you? Dang, my wife and I love that thing.

CHRISTOPH

Well, thank you / so much...

MARY

It is just such fascinating work. So glad you're here. I truly can't believe you're our new panelist. Good job, Charlotte!

CHARLOTTE

I told you I was working on it.

MARY

I didn't know it'd be a bestselling author. Goodness me. Our audiences will be beside themselves.

CHARLOTTE

Alright gang, they're ready in the booth, so it's showtime!

(The "Let It Grow" theme song opening blares into the space.)

MARY

Welcome to another episode. We're so glad you're joining us. As always, we've got a wonderful group with us on the panel today— and we do so look forward to getting to your questions, don't we Charlotte?

CHARLOTTE

So many wonderful topics to cover today, and from all over the state.

MARY

I can't wait to dive in. Of course you all know Charlotte Tradere, who joins us every week to read all of your wonderful messages and help us choose what topics to explore. And next to her is our very own longtime sustainable agriculture expert, Mr. Jeb Alethea.

JEB

Ready for another week, Ms. Mary. Especially now that Mr. Marion / is with us.

MARY

And I was about to introduce—oh my goodness—I am truly astonished, joining our show this week is Dr. Christoph Marion.

CHRISTOPH

It is my absolute pleasure to join the "Let It Grow" family.

MARY

I'm sure our viewers already know, but you're a celebrated horticulturist and author, and truly one of the few scientists in the last decade to create a massive movement in the country by teaching so many who wanted to grow how to do it through understanding propagation and botanical reproduction.

CHRISTOPH

Yes, I was so pleased to find out that so many co-op gardens were started in neighborhoods thanks to my book....

MARY

And the title of this epic tome, my goodness, it just puts a smile on your face.

CHRISTOPH

Fifty Shades of Stamens, yes.

MARY

Fifty Shades of Stamens, how clever!

CHRISTOPH

A title that I did not originate by the way, but I have a very creative publisher who suggested it.

MARY

And the rest is history: a *New York Times* Best Seller. But certainly your ideas on natural processes with parent stock got a lot of people becoming confident gardeners and enthusiasts....

CHARLOTTE

You propagated propagation into the 21st Century!

(They all laugh.)

MARY

Aren't you punny! Heavens.... *(They settle after a good giggle.)* Well, Dr. Marion, we are so delighted you're joining us. Now, Charlotte—what have our friends out there sent us today?

(They reference a monitor off somewhere.)

CHARLOTTE

We're starting today with a lovely tropical plant that so many of us enjoy in our homes. Betsy Conrad of Conway sends us this photo of her beloved Prince of Orange that she's had for five years.

MARY

Will you look at that wonderful, wonderful Philodendron erubescens?

CHRISTOPH

These are stunning plants, and are sometimes a little more costly in retail due to their scarcity.

MARY

They get that regal name from the wonderful yellows and oranges of the new leaves when they first appear.

CHRISTOPH

    Like a new prince being born, or a future potentate peeking through the crack of a boudoir door and glimpsing the unexpected bosom of a young Maid in Waiting behind a changing screen.

MARY

    Thrusting forth with new life—expecting things new and golden.

CHRISTOPH

    Only to be weakened with time, succumbing to the sentence of all life before it—as the sun, that once drew its vigor, now transitions its divinity into the same green that surrounded it at first light.

(Mary and Christoph seem to understand each other, but the poetic assessment has left Jeb and Charlotte speechless. After a spell....)

CHARLOTTE

    Okay...well, Ms. Conrad notes that the tips of her Prince seemed to be rotting away, taking away some of the plants robust luster.

JEB

    Curious...

MARY

    Yes, tell us more...

CHARLOTTE

    Upon further investigation she learned her cat, Droofus—a Maine Coon—was snacking on the plant overnight.

MARY

    Droofus, what a whimsical and fun name.

CHARLOTTE

Ms. Conrad wonders the best pruning plan to restore the Prince of Orange to its regal state.

JEB

Well, before we talk pruning, we should talk about Droofus.

MARY

How so?

JEB

Philodendrons are famously toxic to our furry friends at home. When did we receive this message from Ms. Conrad?

CHARLOTTE

Umm...two weeks ago.

JEB

Oh dear....

MARY

My goodness....

JEB

Well, we'll hope the best for Droofus.

CHRISTOPH

We certainly will. I can offer that damaged Philodendrons will often drop their own leaves after they perish, which will restore vivacious growth afterwards. However, if the leaves have become unsightly it is possible to prune the leaf as long as you're careful not to damage the node.

MARY

We do hope Droofus didn't ingest too much of the Prince, and that he's enjoying his eight remaining lives and resuming his cat-begot curiosity with caution. It's important to remember that plants and pets need a lot of attention, and that it is best to look into the toxicity of our botanical buds before we introduce them to the home.

JEB

Google is out there, so you can also do that before you write into the show. Just a thought.

MARY

Though we do appreciate everyone who shares their questions with us. We'll answer some more after this quick message from our friends and sponsors: The Gardener's Warehouse, and of course, Garden Armory.

("Let It Grow" theme song plays the segment out.)

SCENE III

Some time has passed. Another episode has just wrapped. Mary, Jeb, Christoph and Charlotte are at the garden coach desk. It's very clear something has gone wrong.

CHARLOTTE

I thought we were cooking with gas finally, but no—we have to have another catastrophe!

CHRISTOPH

I don't understand/...?

CHARLOTTE

We're barely halfway through the season, and you have to bring politics into the show?

MARY

Now Charlotte, dear....

CHARLOTTE

We'll lose all of our sponsors with this kind of talk on the show.

MARY

Well he wasn't doing anything but telling the truth, Charlotte.

CHRISTOPH

I mean, I got hired at the University specifically to address this topic.

CHARLOTTE

This isn't an institution of higher learning Mr. Marion. This show is public broadcast. We're already a controversy in this state because of the way we're publicly funded.

CHRISTOPH

I'm really / sorry Charlotte...

CHARLOTTE

You can talk / about weather on here...

MARY

Charlotte, dear, you really need to / take a breath....

CHARLOTTE

You can talk about the historically changing environmental conditions / in the area and that kind of thing....

MARY

Charlotte, please, cooler / heads prevail....

CHARLOTTE

You can talk about quivering pistils for all I care....

CHRISTOPH

I'm sorry if I made / a mistake....

CHARLOTTE

But as soon as you use the words "Global Warming" or "climate change"—we're looking at real trouble. *Real* trouble.

MARY

I think we need to count to ten. Let's be professional, dear.

(Charlotte does not like that. Pause.)

CHRISTOPH

Could we just re-film the segment? We could do it before it airs?

CHARLOTTE

That would be a compelling idea, if we weren't just doing YouTube live! God, the station wants us to do everything we can to be hip and relevant, and it's going to bite us in the ass.

JEB

Just take it off the internet then.

CHARLOTTE

Oh my god, it doesn't work like that. Whoever saw it, saw it. And they could have filmed it, downloaded it, or whatever. And if Gerry saw it, I bet he'll be calling me any minute now. And I don't want to talk to Gerry! I never want to talk to Gerry....

MARY

Goodness, Charlotte, I'll talk to him. I've known the man for years. Never liked him, but I've known him.

CHRISTOPH

I don't think positing that southern plants are migrating north is so controversial.

JEB

The northern ridge of Zone 7 and 8 have already shifted, the trees are doing that on their own.

CHRISTOPH

The USDA has already changed the heartiness zone map.

JEB

It was in the *Washington Post*. You heard of WaPo, Charlotte?

CHARLOTTE

Yes, I read it, Jeb.

JEB

Then I guess you already got that breaking news?

CHARLOTTE

Yes, I know the USDA changed the map. The idea of migrating zones is not the problem. It's the fact that you said "Due to Global Warming," then stated your facts, then editorialized by saying, "we're going to be facing a lot of troubling shifts and transmutations."

CHRISTOPH

/ That's the truth! That. Is. The. Truth.

JEB

If we can't talk about it here, then where can we? It's a show about plants!

CHARLOTTE

Thank God Mary shifted the conversation to azaleas and their shorter bloom periods. That's how you talk about it Mr. Marion. You can be on your soapbox but it better be cute and anecdotal. That's the show!

MARY

I think it's all going to be alright, dear. You're right: that is the show. Let's just...take a breath. There ya go.

CHARLOTTE

Ok...I'll just...take a breath. I just feel like a human shield for this show sometimes. I mean, I know Mr. Goldstein just started supporting the show—and he's pretty left-leaning. Gardner's

Warehouse is committed to sustainability. But Gerry, he's been sponsoring for ten years now—and he thinks his money actually directs the show.

MARY

Well what do you expect from the man who started Garden Armory?

JEB

Garden Armory: the only establishment where pistils and pistols meet.

MARY

Shrubs and shots for the modern American naturalist.

CHARLOTTE

The man's a menace.

(They laugh. Then Charlotte's cell phone rings. She holds it up to see who it is.)

CHARLOTTE

Fuck my life. *(She begins to exit to have a very uncomfortable conversation:)* Hello Mr.... Yes, I know. We were just talking about that very thing. No, I agree....

(A pregnant silence among the remaining coaches. Jeb starts to go after his mic pack in his back pocket.)

JEB

Well, this mic pack was getting uncomfortable on me at the end there.

MARY

You're always wearing overalls, just clip it to the back.

JEB

Then my back would be discomforted. I can't be sitting all funny on the television. I need to be looking as slick as a baby seal covered in motor oil, know what I mean?

MARY

Whatever you say, Jeb.

JEB

And are we broke or something? Godalmighty, I feel like these chairs are gonna give. We can't get something new?

MARY

We're trying to get our money's worth out of them.

(Jeb is purposefully trying to get them to laugh.)

JEB

Well, I believe you done got it. Look at this shit, I feel like I'm on a damn rocking horse.

MARY

You're a mess.

CHRISTOPH

Thanks for the much-needed levity.

(Charlotte re-enters. She picks her big purse up from behind the desk, grabs her smaller purse from inside of it, and throws the big one on top of the desk.)

MARY

What's the story, dear?

CHARLOTTE

Seems Gerry Morus is going to meet with me and Angela in Sponsorships tomorrow to talk to us about the future of his "relationship with the program."

MARY

That's absurd. I'll come with you, Charlotte.

CHARLOTTE

No, you asked me to produce. I can take the shots.

MARY

I've been doing this show for....

CHARLOTTE

Thirty years, I know.

MARY

I'm just saying I can go in with you. Strength in numbers.

CHARLOTTE

No, I'm producing the show, and I'll handle it, love. Okay? Now, I'm going to Dixon's to down a Long Island iced tea. And once I'm done with that, I'll probably have another, 'cause I can't seem to catch a break. You're all welcome to join of course.

JEB

Dixon's it is! Ya'll coming?

CHARLOTTE

Well, actually, Mary has to film in Beaufort tomorrow morning.

MARY

Yes, thank you, maybe not tonight.

(Charlotte takes off, leaving her big bag on the desk.)

JEB

Mr. Marion?

CHRISTOPH

I'd better not. But thank you.

JEB

Aw hell, Mary. I meant to tell you I saw Dale over the weekend.

MARY

You did now?

JEB

Yes mam. He had himself a new girlfriend with him, too.

MARY

Oh yeah?

JEB

Mmm hmmm. I mean, I ain't saying Dale's got an ounce of handsome in him, but godamighy you talk about ugly? His girl could trick or treat over the phone.

MARY

(Laughing:) Stop! I think we should just hope that he's happy, don't you?

JEB

You know I'm just foolin'. I know the ole boy deserves a little happiness. But it's like she caught on fire and someone put her out with a chain.

MARY

Jeb! You're terrible!

JEB

Well, on that I'll say "goodnight." Mr. Marion. Don't ya'll worry about all of this. Gerry will just huff and puff and hiss, but he ain't going to blow this house down. The Hash Tag Jeb Nation loves his store too much. Hash Tag Wink. Hash Tag I'll use my followers to make him file for bankruptcy. See ya'll soon!

(Jeb exits.)

CHRISTOPH

I'm really sorry, Mary.

MARY

Don't you make a fuss about it too. I've always thought it strange that the natural world could be politicized. But here we are.

CHRISTOPH

Here we are.

MARY

I got myself in trouble back when I started the show.

CHRISTOPH

You did?

MARY

I agreed too vehemently with Lawrence Crockett's "Wildly Successful Plants."

CHRISTOPH

Ah, yes—weeds...

MARY

Yes, and I got into the weeds apparently. Made a case for the lacking of herbicides to work on chickpeas and onions and the like, and boy did the retail outlets get angry.

CHRISTOPH

Felt you were dipping into their pockets I take it.

MARY

Home Depot is a force most powerful. Their regional managers watch the show, so we learned.

CHRISTOPH

It's a great show, Mary. You should be proud.

MARY

Thank you. It's been getting harder the past few years, but I'm glad you're on it! Even if you do make Gerry Morus sweat. You know, we should celebrate.

CHRISTOPH

Yeah?

MARY

    Yeah! I mean, I got into sponsor trouble a few shows in. So did you—we might be birds of a feather.

CHRISTOPH

    As long as we're not birds feeding on Nandina berries.

MARY

    Heavenly Bamboo.

CHRISTOPH/MARY

    Toxic.

MARY

    No, we aren't starved birds looking for last resorts. But I do think we could enjoy some berries. Just hold on one second.... *(She fetches a bottle of strawberry wine and glasses from her office upstage. Returns.)* Strawberry wine oughta do the trick. Now I know you didn't want to go to Dixon's / but I thought...

CHRISTOPH

    I just didn't want to go watch Charlotte drink herself feral due to frustration. On account of me that is...

(Mary pours their glasses.)

MARY

    Oh she'll be fine. But it's much quieter here, and you can drink and think. Dixon's always has that music up so loud, it's hard to enjoy company with all that Nickelback.

CHRISTOPH

    Thank you much. *(They sip.)* Wow, well this is....

MARY

Terrible. It's absolutely terrible.

CHRISTOPH

No, now...I wasn't gonna say that.

MARY

Christoph, if there's two things I know its plants and the drinks that come from plants, and this is swill. It cheapens my day.

CHRISTOPH

Ok, maybe you're right.

MARY

I did a segment out at Buck n' Anne's, and they gave me this as a parting gift. Sweet people, but whatever winery in Greer they're shipping their berries off to— goodness, they should be thrown into prison by the taste police.

CHRISTOPH

Bad wine, and good company is still a win in my book.

MARY

I couldn't agree more. To good company. *(They clink glasses, sip, and grimace a bit.)* God, it challenges my uvula. So, beyond all this trouble you're getting us into, how's it been for you living here?

CHRISTOPH

Oh it's fine, you know. Just fine.

MARY

Good.

CHRISTOPH

I've already got a place that's become my regular meat and three visit.

MARY

Edna's over on 123? *(Christoph nods.)* Well, Edna is a dear woman. Her and her husband have been looking over that place for some time now. Used to belong to her daddy. Mr. Bill. He passed ten years ago due to genetic complications.

CHRISTOPH

Oh dear, like Huntington's or Tay-Sachs?

MARY

No, like womanizing. His wife caught him gallivanting, and reintroduced him to his favorite hunting rifle.

CHRISTOPH

Funny how the things you love can wind up killing you.

MARY

That's true. Don't get negligent with your wine there Mr. Marion. We've got a bottle to put out of our misery.

(They sip and grimace.)

CHRISTOPH

You know, there's this little place down the way from there that looks closed that I wish was still open. Its got an Italian flag barely hanging on out front. I looked in the window. Looked like a real cozy place. You know what I'm talking about?

MARY

Oh yeah...yeah, it was called Gino's.

CHRISTOPH

Gino's. Well what happened to it? Looked like a family-owned business too, and I could sure scarf down some Old World recipes.

MARY

Gino was a wonderful man, and his secret was using the freshest herbs. I'm telling you, wasn't a single vegetable or herb in that place that came from a distributor. All straight from the garden.

CHRISTOPH

Mmm...that sounds divine.

MARY

His wife owned a nursery at the time, and she insisted that everything come from her nursery or garden. It was so sweet the way those two worked together. Thick as thieves.

CHRISTOPH

Well, my mouth is watering—and it is not from this unexpected vintage you've served me.

MARY

The place was packed every night. There was always specials, depending on the season. And the food was just made with love, you know? Gino really loved people.

CHRISTOPH

I can't imagine a hospitality business these days where the owner loves people.

MARY

Different times I guess.

CHRISTOPH

So did he pass, or something?

MARY

Gino had a habit of not delegating, you see.

CHRISTOPH

Yep, I know folks like that.

MARY

And he had this habit, every night, thirty minutes before the doors opened. He'd go out and sweep the sidewalk and the parking lot.

CHRISTOPH

Didn't want leaves in his restaurant?

MARY

It was more about giving folks an experience as soon as they arrived. And sure, the leaves would blow back around after things got opened up—but as you were heading home to get your family, you'd be seeing Gino sweeping those leaves up. Felt like he was doing it for you, ya know? To make you welcome once you rounded up the kids and pulled back in. I guess it was just another way of sharing his love.

CHRISTOPH

Got hit by a drunk driver?

MARY

No, he had a heart attack one night. At 4:38 p.m. on a Thursday.

CHRISTOPH

Goodness me...

MARY

He uh, well apparently it couldn't have been expected. He was fairly healthy. Stopped smoking in his 20s. Didn't drink that much. But then...*(snaps)* suddenly, Gino wasn't with us anymore.

CHRISTOPH

That's so sad. I'm sure this community felt his loss.

MARY

They did. Lord knows I did. I wanted to shut down the nursery immediately after it happened. Just looking at them made me miss him too much.

CHRISTOPH

It was your nursery? *(Mary nods.)* He was your husband? *(Mary nods, takes a sip.)* I'm real sorry to hear that. I know that sort of pain is...well, it's endless.

MARY

"Time heals all wounds," isn't that the saying?

CHRISTOPH

Yes....

MARY

That was, goodness, four years ago. Things do get better with time. Here and there. But there's those little reminders and those big reminders. "The price of love is grief."

CHRISTOPH

That's another one of those sayings.

MARY

It sure is. Who's making all these sayings up?

CHRISTOPH

I wish I knew. "We bereaved are not alone. We belong to the largest company in all the world—the company of those who have known suffering." That was Helen Keller. I do know that one.

MARY

Well you pulled that one out of the memory banks.

CHRISTOPH

My wife used to say it all the time. Emily. When she knew she was gonna be sick.

MARY

Emily?

CHRISTOPH

Yeah, she...well, she was diagnosed with early-onset dementia. Brilliant historian, her focus was education in the 20th century. And when Dr. Wells told us she was on a downward slope—she kept bringing that quote up. Tried to make me feel like we were part of a righteous number I guess. But God, did I feel alone.

MARY

When did she pass?

CHRISTOPH

A year and a half ago. So time healing all wounds and all, I just keep looking at the calendar. Is today the day? Am I over it yet? Does it still hurt?

MARY

Of course it does.

CHRISTOPH

Towards the end, I was wishing it could've been something sudden. Something unexpected, you know? Watching her fade away was....

MARY

I can't imagine....

CHRISTOPH

The funny thing is...when I'd find her on the neighbor's porch thinking it was ours, or if she was eating God-knows-what because she didn't know any better—I still just saw that twenty-year-old I fell in love with.

MARY

Mercy....

CHRISTOPH

It's like the past forty years had never happened. I'd just see the same girl who convinced me to hijack her daddy's car so we could go to Folly for the weekend. It was a convertible, and she wanted the top down so her hair could fly all over the place. I loved it, still remember it. And that's who I saw when she was disappearing. And that's what it's like. Trust me. It's like watching someone just fade away. And then you're finally confronted with the truth when they're gone. Feeling like you missed time or something. Like, "well, she was here, why didn't you try to make every moment count if I knew I was going to lose her." I think I've had too much of this strawberry wine Ms. Lily.

MARY

Did you take care of her the best you could Christoph?

CHRISTOPH

I think I did.

MARY

Well there's nothing else you could've done. Large live oaks lose their branches and keep growing towards the sun. The branches return to the soil, creating new life. It's a powerful cycle isn't it?

CHRISTOPH

I'm still a mess....

MARY

In that case, I believe hugs are a powerful thing too. *(She stands up.)* Come here.

(They hug.)

CHRISTOPH

I'm sorry.

MARY

That's alright. It's alright. *(They separate but keep holding each other.)* I can see you in there.

CHRISTOPH

What do you mean?

MARY

Well we're both getting older. But I can see that young man, stealing his girlfriend's daddy's Cadillac—right there in those eyes.

We're still here, so we have to make the most of it. Know what I mean? *(Christoph kisses Mary.)* ...Well, that's not quite what I was meaning....

CHRISTOPH

I'm sorry....

MARY

It's alright....

CHRISTOPH

No, I'm sorry. I shouldn't have. I just....

MARY

Things happen....

CHRISTOPH

I just felt like I knew you suddenly, and that you knew me.

MARY

Yes....

CHRISTOPH

Like we knew each other. What we've been through. And it, well....

MARY

A fleeting moment, I know....

CHRISTOPH

It just felt/...well, it felt....

MARY

It was a feeling and/ it felt....

CHRISTOPH

It felt good. For a fleeting moment, I felt good. Like being somewhere else, other than in my head.

(They pause, then kiss again. With more abandon this time, like teenagers figuring it out.)

MARY

Mr. Marion, I need to show you something in my office. *(She takes off towards the office, back at him....)* Grab the strawberry wine....

(He does so and follows.)

SCENE IV

Time has passed. Still in the studio that night. Mary enters, basically disrobed save for some blanket from the office that she's adorned so that she can, with modesty, retrieve the glasses. Charlotte enters quickly, retrieving her bag from the panel that she left there earlier. She's had a few. The two women see each other and exclaim, startled.

CHARLOTTE

Oh! / Oh my god!

MARY

Goodness! I didn't / know you were....

CHARLOTTE

I forgot my bag. Oh shit, I forgot / my bag....

MARY

I didn't know you were coming back, / goodness me....

CHARLOTTE

I forgot my bag. I forgot my bag, and I came back. Are you naked, in a blanket, Mary?

MARY

I seem to be, yes...close to it. I'm sorry. I didn't think anyone was here.

CHARLOTTE

Caught ya changing before you went home, I guess? Oh I'm sorry, Mary.

MARY

No, now—don't you fret about it. I was just grabbing these glasses and taking them back to the office. Need to clean 'em up before I leave.

CHARLOTTE

Of course you gotta clean your glasses.

MARY

Just, need to get 'em spic and span.

CHARLOTTE

Grabbing your glasses, in a blanket, of course! No problem. Sorry I barged in here unannounced, you're just usually gone. Two glasses? You've got two glasses? Mary, you only drink out of one glasses.

(Christoph appears in the office door. Couch pillow over his part and parcel.)

CHRISTOPH

Is everything alright, Mary?

CHARLOTTE

Is that Mr. Marion?

MARY

Now, Charlotte...

CHARLOTTE

I had two Long Island iced teas, and a margarita, then Jeb stated we must enjoy a Jameson shot to bless the proceedings of the meeting tomorrow because we're gonna lose our sponsor 'cause he's super pissed, so am I seeing Mr. Marion over there in your office doorway with a couch pillow over his part and parcel?

MARY

That might be Mr. Marion over there with a couch pillow over his part and parcel, yes.

CHRISTOPH

The couch pillow was the closest thing to grab when I heard all the ruckus....

CHARLOTTE

To which, you covered up your part and parcel because obviously you're naked and Mary is naked...

MARY

In a blanket...

CHARLOTTE

In a blanket, yes...and I've been drinking and I'm getting my bag. And you're both naked.

MARY

Well, I'm not going to gaslight you and tell you you've had too much to drink....

CHARLOTTE

I have had too much to drink. Obviously.

CHRISTOPH

I do apologize to appear in a doorway in this state...couch pillow over my part and parcel.

CHARLOTTE

No, there's no way I'm seeing what I'm seeing. Because Morus is going to pull his sponsorship tomorrow if I can't assure him that

I'm managing things in a tip-top way, and I've got our much-loved host, Mary Lily, in the studio covered up with a couch blanket while the new panelist on the show is in the office doorway with a couch pillow on his part and parcel after he blew up everything with talk of global warming. Damn it! *Damn it! Damn it!*

MARY

We can explain dear, let's count to ten....

CHARLOTTE

Oh, I'm counting, love. I'm gonna go and count. Yep. *(Charlotte takes her bag and exits quickly:)* One...two... three...four....

(Mary looks back at Christoph and laughs. What a night!)

SCENE V

The next day in Angela's office. Charlotte sits front and center, in what feels like a spot lit interrogation. Mr. Morus and Angela are beyond the fourth wall.

CHARLOTTE

    Mr. Morus. I deeply understand your concerns, and we....

(Interrupted, she listens. Every time there's a line break, Mr. Morus or Angela are speaking.)

    Absolutely, your gift over the years...

    Thank you for correcting me: over the decades.

    Mmm hmmm. Well, we truly have no intention of turning the program into something it shouldn't be. You're right, we shouldn't put ourselves at risk of alienating viewers – and especially not our supporters. Facts not theories from here on out.

    Yes, well, Mr. Marion has already apologized to the entire staff for making the show feel like his classroom, and I'm sure he'd be happy to....

    No, you're right. He's a...well – that word you used.

    Mary? Well, I told her I would express our sincerest apologies over the incident.

    Oh, no she wanted to be here, but I told her that I could handle it as the co-producer....

    When? Well, a little before this season started actually.

    Yes, very new to the position...

(She listens.)

    Well Angela is right. We are going to refrain from live streaming any content until we're confident that Mr. Marion has adapted to his new environment. I certainly expect Ms. Lily to help us with that. Even though she seems to turn a completely blind eye to anything Mr. Marion does. Come to think of it, I'm not sure what it is about him that she so strongly favors. I could use a little transitional support from her, right now. You know what I mean? It's like she's just decided she's on a permanent vacation, or something – while I'm constantly getting thrown in front of firing squads, it feels like. I mean, would it be so hard for her to empower me, like actually empower me, to run things rather than telling me to count? I know how to count. I've been counting since I was a little kid. I may be certified in counting at this point.

(Realizing she got overwhelmed. Mr. Morus chimes in.)

Excuse my forwardness...

What a colorful turn of phrase, Mr. Morus.

Well, that certainly makes me very grateful. I know everyone will be grateful. I'll keep everything under control from here on out. And Angela is here to witness: you have my word.

SCENE VI

The cast is assembled at the desk filming the next show. Mary is wearing a crown made of flowers—something she made herself—and Christoph is beaming at her.

MARY

> We do hope you enjoyed that wonderful visit to Roses Unlimited in Laurens, and Charlotte—we're so pleased you found this delightful spot where all of the plants are certified by the South Carolina Department of Plant Industry over at the university.

CHARLOTTE

> They've been in business for over 35 years, and I just love putting my order in for the spring every year.

MARY

> I've seen your rose bushes, and they are so vivacious and vibrant. Did you get those from Roses Unlimited?

CHARLOTTE

> I sure did.

CHRISTOPH

> Growing roses is such a wonderful way to brighten up any home, and I have found that it becomes extremely helpful when Valentine's Day or an anniversary rolls around—because nothing shows you care like roses you've put your love into.

MARY

> I couldn't agree more. Well Charlotte, maybe you can let me come over and prune a few for a new headpiece sometime?

CHARLOTTE

> Sure....

MARY

Floral haberdashery can be so much fun....

CHRISTOPH

You are just glowing in that headdress today.

MARY

/And I thank you!

JEB

I was going to say, you're looking finer than frog's hair split four ways with that on, Ms. Mary. Looks like you found some anthurium somewhere.

CHARLOTTE

It's about time we check in on messages / from our viewers.

MARY

Well, Mr. Marion and I found this lovely shop on our way back from Laurens earlier in the week.

CHRISTOPH

Coco's Jungle Junction in Joanna.

MARY

Yes, Coco's Jungle Junction in Joanna, and they had an amazing collection of all sorts of wonderful tropical plants. And Jeb, they receive a multifarious shipment every week from Hawaii, and you wouldn't believe your eyes.

JEB

I'd have to see it to believe it.

MARY

You'll have to see it to believe it, for sure.

CHARLOTTE

Our viewers have been seeing some amazing things at their homes that they wanted to share / with us.

MARY

And I can't wait to see them, but I did want to share one of the more precious finds Mr. Marion and I saw at Coco's Jungle Junction—Jeb, you're going to love this. *(To the booth:)* Could ya'll get that photograph up for me?

CHARLOTTE

Wait, I don't have this on my script Ms. Mary.

MARY

A little surprise Charlotte! I was so delighted to see this over the weekend, and I asked Jayden to put this up for us. There it is!

(A picture of a hot lips plant appears.)

CHRISTOPH

Will you look at that.

JEB

I'll be....

MARY

This promiscuous plant is the psychotria elata.

CHRISTOPH

It's earned the name hot lips plant in many circles. And you can see why.

CHARLOTTE

I didn't know we were talking about a psychotria elata on today's program.

MARY

Well, once you've been introduced to one of these in person it's absolutely alluring.

CHRISTOPH

Simply fascinating and magnetic.

MARY

These luscious plants are understory flora in the rainforests of Central and South America—Colombia, Costa Rica, Panama usually. It loves rich soil and humidity.

CHRISTOPH

You definitely want to keep these in a place where you'll have indirect light and plenty of moisture. They really do love an environment that mimics the floor of the rainforest—somewhere sultry.

MARY

Sultry and steamy is best for the elata.

CHARLOTTE

Well that's definitely interesting / but...

MARY

And what makes these so fun is that when they bloom, their petals look like these. Like lips with red lipstick on.

JEB

I believe I've heard the colloquial name for psychotria elata more than I've heard "hot lips plant." Not sure we can say it on this program.

CHARLOTTE

Don't say it on this program.

JEB

Shakespeare would say strumpet's lips. But instead of strumpet which rhymes with trumpet, most people say something that rhymes with "looker" if you get my meaning. Looker's lips.

MARY

Yes, and the elata certainly makes you want to pucker up and kiss it.

CHRISTOPH

Some creatures do kiss it, like hummingbirds, which are its pollinators, but also many species of butterflies and bees. These fascinating flowers are a valuable part of the ecosystem with so many stops along the circle of life. After they move beyond the "lips" phase of blooming, they grow smaller flowers inside—which the hummingbirds so enjoy. And then, after that the flowers develop into blueberries—which feeds many types of birds all year long.

MARY

Georgia O'Keeffe would have loved to paint this.

JEB

Well, if we're getting into suggestive plants....

CHARLOTTE

    We're not.

JEB

    My wife has been spending the past year diving into fungicultures, and she has had some great luck with yielding Phallus Impudicus. And the scientific name fits too. But most people call them common stinkhorn.

MARY

    I could go back to Coco's and get the elata, and you could bring one of your stinkhorns and we could see what happens.

(They all laugh except for Charlotte, who is obviously mortified.)

JEB

    Now you're talking.

CHRISTOPH

    Watch out, those "looker's" lips may get stuck on that stinkhorn and we'll get into trouble with the FCC for graphic horticulture.

MARY

    I can't believe she got those to grow. That's such a Western variety.

JEB

    What can I say, my love is a fine fungiculturalist.

MARY

    That's truly wonderful. Well, Charlotte—let's see what our viewers have sent into us this week.

CHARLOTTE

Unfortunately...that's all the time we have for today's program.

MARY

Well, I do hope you'll all excuse our divergence this week. When we see something so extraordinary we do like to show it on the program, and hope you enjoy it as much as we do.

CHARLOTTE

As always, we want to thank Garden Armory and Gardner's Warehouse for sponsoring this program, along with support from viewers like you.

MARY

Yes, thanks to you, and thanks to our sponsors—we'll see you next time on "Let It Grow."

(Music plays the show out. The cast take their mics off during the following, except for Charlotte, who just exits suddenly. Maybe to count to ten.)

MARY

Y'all are a mess!

JEB

Every now and then, we get to have a little goof or two on here. Keeps us young Ms. Mary!

MARY

Speak for yourself! Oh goodness....

CHRISTOPH

We need to go back to Coco's in the near future I think.

MARY

I'd love to! The cyclomens there were absolutely gorgeous, and I need to replace mine after last winter's freeze. Poor dears just bent over and died.

(Christoph begins to stand.)

CHRISTOPH

You've got the entire Garden of Eden over there. Something is bound to not make it. Now if ya'll will pardon me—nature has been calling since we started taping. See what I did there?

MARY

Nature! Goodness!

(Christoph exits.)

JEB

Now, how come Christoph got an invitation over to the Lily estate and I didn't.

MARY

Well…you probably wouldn't believe it. But what if I told you that Mr. Marion and I are enjoying the kindling of a new relationship together?

JEB

I'd say that would make me very happy for you two.

MARY

Then be happy then.

JEB

You for real?

MARY

I am!

JEB

Betsy is going to keel over when I tell her. That's just damn lovely, Ms. Mary. Now you know if he hurts you I'm gonna have to break him in like a new deck of cards.

MARY

I'm sure he already knows that. He knows you look out for me.

JEB

Yes mam. Well good on ya. Good on ya both. Happy for you.

MARY

Thank you much.

JEB

You better be careful bringing him over to your yard though.

MARY

Why's that?

JEB

That neighbor of yours? Clara Dean?

MARY

You hush now...

JEB

I saw Clara Dean heading to church one Sunday when I was driving by. Girl should be ashamed wearing what she was wearing. Her pants were so tight she could have fart and blew her boots off.

MARY

Well, you can come over to the house right now if you want to. You can protect Mr. Marion from himself.

JEB

Well how 'bout it? I think I'll do just that.

(Mary and Jeb laugh as Christoph returns.)

MARY

Were your ears burnin'?

CHRISTOPH

Might've been. Well, we heading out?

MARY

Yes, and Jeb is joining us.

CHRISTOPH

Well that sounds like a bit of alright. I've got a bottle of Pappy over there too, if you want a sip?

JEB

Does Dolly Parton sleep on her back? *(They start to leave. Charlotte returns. Jeb collects the mics to give to her.)* Hold on. Gotta pay the toll.

CHARLOTTE

You can give the mics to Jayden.

JEB

Alright. Is there any reason you look like you were expecting a bottle of champagne and instead it was a jug of buttermilk?

CHARLOTTE

Just give them to Jayden. I don't have to do everything for everyone. Take care of yourselves.

JEB

Yes mam. Damn, no need to be sandpaperin' my ass.

(Jeb exits. Christoph and Mary are about to leave as well.)

CHRISTOPH

See you over there, Jeb. *(To Mary:)* I'm going to drop by my house and get that Fleetwood Mac record I promised you.

MARY

Don't threaten me with a good time. *(To Charlotte:)* You wanna come over to the house, dear?

(Charlotte waits until Christoph has left.)

CHARLOTTE

Are you two having a full-on relationship, Mary?

MARY

Well, I don't see why that's anyone's business.

CHARLOTTE

At work it is somebody's business. It's my business. Have you registered it with HR?

MARY

I'm sorry about the other night, Charlotte. I thought it was just a funny thing that happened, and I knew / you'd understand...

CHARLOTTE

Have you spoken to HR or not?

MARY

No. Why would I?

CHARLOTTE

Well you obviously didn't read our personnel policies very well. Because / if you did...

MARY

I read them. Scanned them / is probably more truthful.

CHARLOTTE

Because if you did read the new personnel policies that Legal gave us two months ago, you would know it clearly states that inter-office relationships need to be reported to Human Resources.

MARY

Well, I'm sorry Charlotte. I guess I've been so caught up in finding a little light at the end of my tunnel that I failed to consult the manual for a job I've been doing for thirty years now.

CHARLOTTE

Would you listen to me please? You need to let them know. We have to do things by the book.

MARY

"By the book" Who's writing this book? My goodness, why does everything have to be so difficult...

CHARLOTTE

I can't keep protecting everyone all the time. Things are different. It's not the 90s anymore.

MARY

Believe me, I know.

CHARLOTTE

And I'm not going to put my ass out on the line, get fired or whatever, because you can't be a professional.

MARY

If this job is becoming too much for you to handle, perhaps we should consider targeting your focus on one aspect or the other. Garden coach or producer. I don't want you to be overwhelmed. And I'm not going to run to Human Resources and claim something, get some paperwork on it, and then have to go back and update them if life goes in a painful direction. Which it invariably does. So no, I'm not keen to follow some new rules that I didn't sign up for after thirty of years of creating one of this station's highest rated programs. And thirty years of an internal culture, come to think of it.

CHARLOTTE

Mary, you signed the personnel manual....

MARY

Actually, I didn't.

CHARLOTTE

You what?

MARY

Because I didn't like a lot of things in it that require me to treat my fellow workers like they don't live lives every day. I'm sorry you don't see it that way. I'm pretty sure our little trips to Dixon's aren't in line with the "policies." But after thirty years, I know we need to decompress after we've put on a show—because, even after thirty years, the adrenaline rushes. We'd be tossing and turning all night if we took off straight to home and crawled into bed. So please. Just count to ten, Charlotte. Do yourself a favor. Do us all a favor. You're welcome to come over to the house, but if not—I'll see you on Monday. Just a few more days of taping then we can all get a much-needed break.

(Mary leaves—leaving Charlotte to breathe heavily and angrily.)

SCENE VII

Mary and Christoph are pruning shrubs. It's a day off, lovely outside, and they're enjoying their time together.

CHRISTOPH

These are some wonderful Beautyberries.

MARY

I do so enjoy them. They were here when we moved in. I didn't have the heart to put something else in.

CHRISTOPH

I used to eat the berries of these when I was growing up. I had a few too many one day and was sick as a dog for a night.

MARY

Goodness.

CHRISTOPH

Yeah, my momma told me I couldn't go around eating everything—even if it was pretty.

MARY

Good advice to be certain. The birds sure do love these. They make my car look like a Pollack painting every spring.

CHRISTOPH

A little clip here.... You know, I was talking about pruning and the possible emotional conditioning of plants in my class last week.

MARY

Oh yes....

CHRISTOPH

And this freshman, young kid from Pelion, well they were / shocked when I mentioned...

MARY

They? I thought this was one student.

CHRISTOPH

Yes, they are "they."

MARY

I see, sorry....

CHRISTOPH

Well they were rather taken with the fact that when you prune improperly that the plant will callous up. Like a scar.

MARY

They sure do. Learn that the hard way when you're starting out.

CHRISTOPH

And so they asked me, "how far does this go?" And I said, "What do you mean?" And they said "Well, how much are plants like humans? How much do they heal or feel, like?" And I had to sit and think on it for a minute.

MARY

Goodness, the emotional complexity of plants conversation. Is that a first-year topic?

CHRISTOPH

I've never had the question come up. But then I thought, and I said, "The Mimosa pudica."

MARY

The touch-me-not.

CHRISTOPH

I said, "The Mimosa pudica can adapt and learn. You can touch it and it will shrivel up, 'cause it thinks that's a danger. Something innate in the plant's complex natural system has learned to protect itself from danger." And I said, "You can start to touch these things regularly and they'll learn that you're safe. That you don't mean them any harm." Compared it to a rescue dog from an abusive home. You know, at first, they think everything is dangerous—and rightly so.

MARY

Well, yes.

CHRISTOPH

But, over time, they realize that you're offering them love and they can go to parks and stuff and play with other dogs and all that. Much like the Mimosa pudica. It just takes time, but it'll feel that there's love out there for it—and it will adapt and change.

MARY

Isn't that lovely.

CHRISTOPH

It is. Well, Solaris just begins to break down and cry right in front of me.

MARY

Oh, the poor dear.

CHRISTOPH

And, they look at me and say, "even the natural world has to learn love is safe." And I was beside myself.

MARY

I can imagine.

CHRISTOPH

I mean really beside myself. I remembered after Emily passed, her peace lilies wouldn't even perk up when I watered them. It's like they were feeling me walking around the house, being all limp. If I wasn't going to perk up, neither were they.

MARY

Same story with my prayer plants. They just stopped doing what they do.

CHRISTOPH

Well...all that's to say, I've been feeling pretty perked up, Mary. And I thank you for it.

MARY

You know, I have too. It's pretty nice isn't it?

CHRISTOPH

Sí, mi amor.

MARY

Now we have romantic languages...?

(Christoph very genuinely and sweetly kisses Mary on the lips. She touches him afterward and smiles. Her phone rings.)

MARY

Now, who would be calling me on a day off?

(Christoph keeps a hold on her.)

CHRISTOPH

Aw now come on, don't go walking away. We got pruning to do.

MARY

You are a handful Mr. Marion. Let me take this.

CHRISTOPH

"I know a bank where the wild thyme blows,
Where oxlips and the nodding violet grows...."

MARY

Oh, you better stop!

CHRISTOPH

"Quite over-canopied with luscious woodbine,
With sweet musk-roses and with eglantine."

MARY

It's the station, Christoph. Put the Shakespeare on hold.

CHRISTOPH

Fine ma lady, take thine call. And make haste for I have more pruning and poetry.

(Christoph playfully releases her and bows. He continues pruning, while she answers the call:)

MARY

Hello? ...Yes, how are you? I must admit I wasn't expecting any calls today, so I'm sorry I kept you listening to that ringer.

Yes? Oh.

Don't speak to anyone from the show? I'm not sure I quite understand.

Well, we're in the middle of taping.

Well, I have to swing by – well, that can wait I guess. Yes, I will see you tomorrow then. Fine. At the studio? No, over there, alright. Yes, I can make it. That's fine. Goodbye.

(She hangs up.)

Something is happening....

(Christoph comforts Mary as she is obviously confused and upset.)

SCENE VIII

Mary slowly enters from her office. It is late and the studio is in the dark. She has a box of her belongings, and she comes to the garden coach desk. Puts her box on it and looks around. Charlotte enters.

CHARLOTTE

Mary...I just heard.

MARY

You just heard, or you just expected?

CHARLOTTE

I just heard.

MARY

I see....

CHARLOTTE

I didn't mean for this to happen.

MARY

Well it did, didn't it? I really wish you weren't here. I'd like to say goodbye alone.

CHARLOTTE

I rushed over here when Legal called me.

MARY

Ya'll must be good friends at this point.

CHARLOTTE

Oh no, it's quite the opposite!

MARY

    Probably be hanging out at Dixon's with them in the near future. Ya'll can sing along to the hits of Nickelback.

CHARLOTTE

    They've put me under a microscope. Lately, it's been feeling like I'm coming to work and I'm literally inside a tornado dream. I just felt…I've just been feeling uncomfortable with everything, you know?

MARY

    No, I don't know. I thought we were family…or something ridiculous like that.

CHARLOTTE

    Mary….

MARY

    You cried at Jeb's mother's bedside. You cried. We all did. You were two months an intern / and I saw you….

CHARLOTTE

    What does that have to do with anything?

MARY

    I saw you cry at Jeb's mother's bedside. You and me, and Dale and Jeb. Watching him endure that pain, and I thought you were part of the family. You seemed to care about the people in the room.

CHARLOTTE

    I did care. I do care. But…I mean work should be work, it shouldn't be a family.

MARY

Well, it should come with some understanding at least—some compassion. A pithy pinch of allegiance to those who are part of your upward climb. And I haven't brought it up, but I'm pretty sure you're the one who told them Dale was having a drinking problem.

CHARLOTTE

I...I don't have....

MARY

Don't have anything to say? Because it's the truth? Did you know Dale was going through a divorce, Charlotte?

CHARLOTTE

I didn't know....

MARY

Did you know that his wife left him for his younger brother? The man lost his entire family in one conversation at home one night? *(Snaps.)*

CHARLOTTE

No, I didn't know.

MARY

Of course you didn't. Because it's not convenient to consider the entire portrait of a person, is it? What they're going through. How they were raised. How they watched others deal with grief before them. How they figure out how to deal with it once they're confronted with it. It's just uncomfortable, isn't it?

CHARLOTTE

I am and have been totally devoted to you, Mary.

MARY

Devoted. So much so that you couldn't talk to me? Do you trust the lawyers more? Do you think they care about you, Charlotte? I trusted you.

CHARLOTTE

I trusted you too.

MARY

And how did I betray your trust?

CHARLOTTE

I was just...you and Mr. Marion were making me uncomfortable. You haven't been listening to me either, and I'm getting hit from all sides by the station. I mean, did you know I was crying in the broom closet last Friday after we shot?

MARY

Why would you hide like that?

CHARLOTTE

Because I had to? Because I couldn't not cry, and I didn't want to make anyone feel uncomfortable.

MARY

Uncomfortable, uncomfortable, uncomfortable. Life is a continual series of discomforts, Charlotte. I thought you could just talk to me.

CHARLOTTE

I tried to talk to you!

MARY

You condescended to me. That's what you did.

(The next two waterfalls of dialogue happen simultaneously, with neither one stopping to listen to the other.)

CHARLOTTE

Me condescend to *you*? Oh my god, let's talk about condescension, please! You've been making it clear that I'm not doing this job as good as you used to do it. I get it: it's your show, it's your show, it's your show, it's your show, it's your show, it's your show, Mary. These asshole lawyers keep telling me the show can't be ran like a circus. Can't be ran like a circus. It can't be ran like a circus, Ms. Tradere, could you do your fucking job and manage the circus, please? Look what I've done? Look what I've done? Look what you've done! This is you! This is you! This is all you! It's all you, love.

MARY

Telling me what *I have to do*, after I built this from the ground up you understand. Thirty years of my life here in this box. Oh please, I have praised you, Charlotte. I have thanked you, Charlotte. I have promoted you, Charlotte. I have tried to take things off of your overwhelmed anxiety-ridden plate, Charlotte. And somehow, here I am being told to leave. You didn't think this through. You didn't think. You didn't think about anything but yourself, and look! Look what you've' done! You didn't think about it for one second. You didn't think! Look what you've done, dear!

CHARLOTTE

/ Don't call me dear.

MARY

Oh, don't call me love.

(They catch their breath.)

CHARLOTTE

I didn't want to lose this.

MARY

You could have said you felt your job was on the line. You could have said that. I would have listened to *that*. Listen, I'm a human. A human perfectly capable of making mistakes. I've always known that.

CHARLOTTE

I didn't know where to turn.

MARY

You could have turned to me. That's all I want you to know at this point. I wanted so much for you. I keep looking around, looking at how this place has looked since we moved here twenty years ago. It's all a fog. It doesn't seem real right now. I guess I'm in shock.

CHARLOTTE

I didn't expect them to let you go. Oh my God, in the middle of the season. This is all fucked.

MARY

(Breathes, then with sincerity:) I'm sorry, Charlotte. I'm sorry that you didn't feel like you were in control, and I'm sorry that you didn't feel comfortable with me and Mr. Marion. Goodness knows I didn't intend for anything to happen—not here—guess I just welcomed some spontaneity for once. I'm sorry that you got overwhelmed. I really am. You always wanted me to let you take care of it, so I was trying to let you take care of it. I thought that's what you wanted. I'm sorry I didn't help you when you needed me to. I'm sorry, Charlotte.

CHARLOTTE

Thank you.

MARY

So now you have your apology from me. I was so lonely, you know? I've been missing Gino so much, and I thought you understood that. When you became a garden coach, I was deep in that grief. You saw me through the worst of it. And Christoph made me feel like me again. I don't know what'll come of it, but I felt home again. It just, well, it felt comfortable.

CHARLOTTE

And I want that for you.

MARY

This show has been my life. Can I have my final moment alone in here? Let's just call it a draw. Me and my sad box deserve it, I think?

CHARLOTTE

Yes. Of course. *(Charlotte turns to leave. Turns back.)* I'll look after the show, Mary. I swear I will. For you.

MARY

What show, Charlotte? This show is over. They may re-imagine it, put some other host and panel in—do all kinds of things to make it modern and what not. YouTube live it. But this show is over.

CHARLOTTE

Over?

MARY

Do you know where "Let it Grow" came from? My grandparents owned a nursery called Let It Grow, and they passed it on to my daddy, then he passed it on to me. Then I started doing segments on Pauly's Six-O- Eight AM. It was called "Let It Grow" and it was all mine. Then Daryl Cornelius wanted to give me a full-on show here on the public channel in 1994. He had no objection to me owning the name of the show, since it was the name of my grandparent's nursery. And I still own it. Even as I walk out those doors with a box full of three decades of trinkets and photos—"Let It Grow" is still mine. Legal understands that too, even if they just see me as a liability. So, you may still produce a show for naturalists. But this show, the one that I hosted on this channel, is over. I don't think Mr. Marion or Jeb are keen to continue on at this station either, at least not according to the last conversation we had. It is a pity that some discomfort should make such a big wave. Could have been a ripple. Especially with the ratings going up with the addition of Christoph. I'll give credit where it's due. That was some good producing, Charlotte.

CHARLOTTE

Thank you.

MARY

Losing the "fight for your family" aspect that we built over three decades is quite the opposite. You want to be comfortable? You got it. You can fight every day to be comfortable, but there will be very few who will help you with it unfortunately. Give it some time. You'll have someone watching every move you make and waiting for you to make a mistake. Apparently that's all that's important now. It's just not the world I was trying to create. Not inclined to pursue it either.

CHARLOTTE

I am sorry. I'm sorry.

MARY

And now I have my apology from you. So maybe we can both count to ten. Now will you please leave me to say goodbye?

(Charlotte, totally broken, nods and leaves.)

SCENE IX

The "Let It Grow" theme song plays, now differently arranged. The studio is now a slicker high-end operation. Mary, with headdress, Christoph and Jeb, having ditched the overalls for actual pants and a shirt, sit at a desk that seems familiar, but nicer.

MARY

Welcome to "Let It Grow!" I'm Mary Lily, and we're so glad you're joining us today as we explore the world of horticulture and botany here on HGTV. With me is a longtime colleague and friend, Mr. Jeb Alethea.

JEB

Good to be here on HGTV Ms. Lily!

MARY

Aren't you looking sharp? And to my immediate left is my fiancé, author and educator Mr. Christoph Marion.

CHRISTOPH

I can't wait to spend another day in the garden with you.

MARY

We're clear proof that second chances are possible. After thirty years on public television, we're so glad to join a national audience to talk about Southern plants and how to give them all the potential they deserve. Now...let's have some fun letting it grow!

END

The Jasper Project Board of Directors 2024

Wade Sellers, President
Kristin Cobb, Vice President
Rebekah Rice, Managing Director
Emily Moffitt, Secretary
Christina Xan, Treasurer
Jon Tuttle, Play Right Series Director
Al Black
Kwasi Brown
Libby Campbell-Turner
Kimber Carpenter
Bert Easter
Loli Molina Munoz
Keith Tolen
Cindi Boiter, Founder and Executive Director

www.ingramcontent.com/pod-product-compliance
Lightning Source LLC
Chambersburg PA
CBHW061803070526
44586CB00023B/2690